This b number five out of seven. It has been written in the eye of 10-year-old Brooke May

In memory of my dad

Chapter one: Brooke's home

"Brooke, darling. Tea's ready?" Asked Mrs Sanderson.

Brooke May was playing on her PlayStation when she heard her mum shouting from downstairs.

Martha Sanderson,

Brooke's older sister knocked on the door and came in without waiting for a reply from me.

"Tea's ready B. What are you playing?" Asked Martha "well I'm playing the game where I am a character who is myself and this other character is called Madison. We've just met a bear called Zoe who is from Japan and her friends

Lily, Star, Rosie, Josie, Chocolate Fudge and Chocolate who is Zoe's brother" I said "wow sounds like a great game Bea. Isn't Madison the girl you met on holiday last year?" Asked Martha as we walked together downstairs. "Yeah, I hope she's okay. I haven't heard from her for a while" I said as we reached the kitchen.

Lily and Martha smiled at me and smiled.

At the Nicholas house, Maddison was on her

PlayStation, playing a game where she was the main character who looks exactly like Maddie, and a bear called Zoe and another girl character called Brooke.

That's when Hannah came into my bedroom and looked around her little sister's room and no teddy's were found just loads of bin bags.

"Mads, what's all this?" Asked Hannah "what do you mean?" I Asked pausing the game "there aren't any teddy's" said Hannah "I know Hannah-Banana" I said "so?" Asked Hannah "oh, grandma" I stopped. I stopped and Hannah knew exactly what I meant "right" said Hannah starting to get up "that's it" Hannah added and about to go downstairs. "Wait where are you going?" I asked. "I am just going downstairs" said

Hannah not wanting to have Maddie guess what she was going to do.

I looked worried at my sister.

Meanwhile, back at the Sanderson house.

Brooke was still playing her game with her sister Martha when her mum came in.

"Girls, it's time for tea" said Mrs Sanderson then she came over to see what we were doing "what are you both doing?" Asked Mrs Sanderson then she looked at her game.

"That looks like you B, isn't Maddie the girl you met on holiday?" Asked Mrs Sanderson "yeah, she gave

me her teddy"
said Brooke
picking up Zoe
and smiled at her
mum "have you
heard anything
from her at all?"
Asked Mrs
Sanderson "yeah,
I'm talking to her

in the game right now?" I said "how?" Asked Mrs Sanderson looking at me strange.

I looked at her "technology mum. Didn't you say tea

was ready?"
Asked Martha
"yeah I did" said
Mrs Sanderson
and we all went
downstairs, and I
left the game still
playing not
knowing what was
going to happen.

While I was downstairs, having tea, a large figure that had blonde hair, and wore a pink T-shirt with a flower that was in the centre, and wore trousers with trainers pop out of the monitor that was connected to the PlayStation and the figure looked around Brooke's room.

Back at the Nicholas house, Hannah walked downstairs, and into the kitchen and over to her parents.

"Mum?" Asked Hannah "yes

darling?" Asked
Mrs Nicholas
"have you noticed
anything different
with Maddie?"
Asked Hannah
"not really love,
why? I can't
believe she's
going to be 16

tomorrow" Asked Mrs Nicholas "she's throwing away all of her teddys," said Hannah.

Mrs Nicholas looked at Hannah "why?" Asked Mrs

Nicholas "why? Why do you think? How do you think has got to her?" Asked Hannah "who?" Asked Mrs Nicholas "grandma" said Hannah "we've

got to stop her"
said Mrs Nicholas
"I don't know yet
but we will think
of something.
Let's just get her
party over first.
Oh god, I can't
wait to see her
face tomorrow

morning" said Mrs Nicholas smiling at Hannah.

Chapter two – Madison turns 16

The early morning of my sixteen birthday, it was 6am and I was woken up by some loud singing. I opened one eye and looked up and saw Hannah, my mum, my dad, Steven, my aunt Hilda, and my cousin Rosie. I smiled at them all and they smiled at me.

"Happy birthday darling," said Mrs Nicholas. I sat up and looked over at Grandma Elizabeth and frowned.

"Where's grandad?" getting out of bed and put my dressing grown and slippers on "he says happy birthday darling. He's just out of town now" said

Grandma Elizabeth "right" said Maddie sounding cold and on edge with Grandma Elizabeth.

Back at the Sanderson' house,

I came up to her bedroom. I looked around and frowned.

"What on earth happened?" I asked looking around my room.

Lily and Martha came up and walked in.

They looked around "what happened?" asked Lily and we walked over to the window.

We looked outside there was no ladder.

"There's no ladder" said Martha "I don't get it" I said, "how can someone get in without a ladder?" I asked "girls, can you come downstairs a minute please?" shouted Mrs Sanderson from downstairs.

Martha, Lily and I all looked at each other confused and started walking downstairs. My mum caught us coming downstairs.

"Martha, darling. Can I have a word with you please?" asked Mrs Sanderson "yeah sure" said Martha looking at me and Lily and followed our mum into the hallway then

Martha saw a figure with blonde hair and then a face and realized it was Maddie's (B's best friend).

"Okay so we've managed to get Maddie down for

a visit" said Mrs Sanderson "oh, that's who got in, just now" said Martha "what do you mean?" asked Mrs Sanderson "we thought someone had broken in but when we went to see outside, there was no ladder" said Martha "anyway what was the question?" asked Martha "could you and lily cover B's eyes and walk her to the kitchen but wait until I say okay, we're not ready yet" said Mrs Sanderson "okay, we will. What is it about?" asked Martha "we're going on holiday with

Maddie and her family" said Mrs Sanderson "omg. That's lush, B's going to love it. It's going to be so fun mum" said Martha "Maddie also doesn't know it's her 16th birthday present from us" said Mrs Sanderson "oh I see, got you" said Martha and she walked back to me and lily "what did mummy want?" I asked, "nothing B, don't worry," said Martha.

Lily looked at Martha and texted Lily.

"Madison is here to surprise B and mum and dad

along with Maddie's mum and dad have booked and paid for a holiday" texted Martha and pressed sent.

Lily looked up at her older sister

Martha smiling as we walked into the kitchen covering Brooke's eyes.

30-45 minutes later, I had still had my eyes closed.

"Can I open them now?" I asked.

Mrs Sanderson was smiling at me and holding up a cardboard sign with the help of her husband and

Maddie's older sister Hannah.

"Yes" said Mrs Sanderson.

I opened my eyes, saw the cardboard sign

that had big writing on:

WE ARE GOING ON HOLIDAY"

"What are you talking about?" I asked.

My mum looked
at me.

"What mum?" I
asked, "close your
eyes" she said
"again?" I asked.
She nodded.

I closed my eyes.

There was silence "okay sweetie, open them," said Mrs Sanderson.

I opened my eyes and there stood Maddison. I

looked surprised and I ran up to Madison "OMG, how" I said, "I'm going on holiday with you B," said Maddie.

Then my mum, my dad, Mrs and

Mr Nicholas came up and looked at Maddie.

"What?" asked Maddie.

"HAPPY SIXTEEN BIRTHDAY MADDIE" shouted

both parents and Mrs Sanderson gave Maddie a birthday card with a note inside.

Maddie read the note out loud.

"To Madison-
Rose,

We would like to
wish a very happy
sixteen birthday
to you and this
gift is for you from
the bottom of our
hearts and we

hope you have a
fantastic day and
enjoy this:

You are going on
holiday with us.
We've booked
and paid for a
holiday for all of
us" Madison

finished reading and looked up at my mum and dad and squeezed them so hard then looked at me.

"We're going on holiday B," said Madison

Chapter four – I don't need them

"Why would you think that?" asked Hannah.

Maddie went silence.

"Mads, what's going on?" asked Hannah as we both sat down on my bed next to Maddie, but she couldn't speak because they heard shouting from downstairs.

"Girls, it's time to go," shouted Mr Nicholas.

Maddie looked at Hannah.

And they held each other's hands with their bags and suitcases and walked downstairs.

"You ready to go?" asked Mrs Nicholas "yeah" said Maddie and Hannah smiling together.

"Let's go then" said Mr Nicholas and he carried

one of the suitcases to the car and opened the boot of the car and Mrs Nicholas with the other and Maddie and Hannah got into the car.

And Mrs and Mr Nicholas got into the car, and he started the engine.

Me and my family were on the same time as Maddie and her family, and my phone beeped to tell her she had a text from Maddie.

My face light up then froze "what is it?" asked Lily. I read it and my face turned from happy to sad.

"What's up B?" asked Martha as we got to St Meryl's "Maddie" I said "yeah, what's happened?" asked Lily "she doesn't

believe anymore"
I said.

"Believe? Believe
in what? What do
you mean?" asked
Lily.

As I was about to speak, Maddie and Hannah came over.

Maddie and Hannah smiled.

"You alright?" asked Hannah.

Lily and Martha looked at me.

I looked at Brooke. She dragged me over to a tree.

"Mads, what's going on? What did you mean by that text?" I asked, "what do you mean?" I asked "exactly what it says, I don't believe anymore. When you go and see Zoe, please don't ask me to come with you. I don't want to see the stupid bear," said Maddie and went off leaving me confused and upset.

Hannah saw everything and me upset and came over "what's up B" asked Hannah "can we go and see Zoe?" I asked "of course. Is Maddie being a teenager again?" asked Hannah. I nodded.

Chapter five – This is your fault

While Hannah and I was going to Crystal Woods. Maddie's grandmother turned up.

"Mum, what are you doing here?" asked Mrs

Nicholas "my granddaughter" said Elizabeth "yeah, Hannah's not here" said Maddie "where is she?" asked Grandma Elizabeth "I don't know" Maddie lied "really?" asked Grandma Elizabeth.

Mrs Nicholas looked at her mum "Can I have a word?" asked Mrs Nicholas "okay Sophie" said Grandma Elizabeth and they went to a tree.

"This is your fault" said Mrs Nicholas "what's my fault Sophie?" asked Grandma Elizabeth "Maddie not believing anymore" said Mrs Nicholas "Good, she is sixteen anyway and off to college soon. It's about time she grew up" said Grandma Elizabeth "you're unbelievable. I can't believe you said that" said Mrs Nicholas.

Meanwhile, as Hannah and I reached Crystal Woods and we stopped when we saw Zoe having a conversation with another a bear.

We reached Zoe and smiled. The bear suddenly looked up and ran.

"Hey, who's that?" I asked "oh, that was Tiger-lily. She's new to the woods, there's also Mint Sauce, leopard and Stripes," said Zoe.

I smiled at Zoe.

"Where's Maddie?" asked Zoe "being a teenager" said Hannah as we started walking further into the woods and it began snowing.

"Teenager?" asked Zoe "what's a teenager?" asked Zoe "well, she's stopped believing for one," said Hannah.

Zoe stopped shocked but we kept walking and turned around and saw Zoe's stunned face.

"What's wrong?" I asked "she stopped

believing? In me? Why?" asked Zoe

"My Grandmother, although she's got no right to anyway because you used to belong to her," said Hannah.

Zoe was so stunned that she could hardly talk "we must put our minds together and come up with a plan" said Zoe finding her voice.

Hannah and I looked at our friend.

Back at St Meryl's Grandma Elizabeth and Sophie came over to Maddie, Michael, Mrs and

Mr Sanderson with Martha and Lily and there stood uncle Gabriel and Rosie, Aunt Hilda, and Maddie's Grandad.

Sophie and Grandma Elizabeth looked confused.

"Hilda!" Sophie cried "Aunt Hilda, Rosie and Uncle Gabriel. What are you doing here?"

asked Maddie smiling.

"we had a call from Hannah. Where is she anyway?" asked Hilda.

Mrs Nicholas looked at her mum unimpressed.

Chapter six – Hannah says

"What do you mean Hannah

called you?"
asked Grandma
Elizabeth "she
informed us
what's been going
on?" said Aunt
Hilda "like what?"
asked Grandma
Elizabeth "that
the truth about

our childhood has been told" said Aunt Hilda.

Back in Crystal Woods, Hannah, Brooke, and Zoe all had a plan to get Maddie back to her believing in Zoe again.

"Right, so we all know the plan?" asked Hannah.

Zoe and I nodded.

"Okay" said Hannah

Back at the campsite, Grandma Elizabeth was looking at both of her daughters.

"I don't know what you're talking about" said Grandma Elizabeth.

My grandad looked at his wife.

"Liz don't lie. It's the truth," said Grandad.

Grandma Elizabeth looked at her husband.

"Okay, fine but I honestly thought I

was doing the right thing, by taking Zoe away from you Sophie, and then Hannah found her, and I felt like I had to do something then Maddie and it's not my fault that Maddie has stopped believing. Maybe it's a good thing" said Grandma Elizabeth.

Sophie and Michael looked at

Grandma Elizabeth.

Cousin Rosie was shocked at her Grandma.

"How can you say that Grandma? That's like you've

ripping Hannah's, Maddie's and Aunt Sophie and my mum's heart out and I know the reason" said Cousin Rosie.

Grandma Elizabeth looked

at Maddie's cousin.

"And what do you think the reason is Rosie?" asked Grandma Elizabeth "your childhood," said Rosie.

"What do you mean?" asked Grandma Elizabeth.

Back in Crystal Woods, Hannah, Brooke, and Zoe

were with the other animals.

"Okay so I phone Maddie saying, "I've had a fall" and you, Zoe meets her at the entrance and get the truth out of her which is obviously Grandma Elizabeth, but Maddie is stubborn and has been lying to us and this whole thing has been about Grandma's childhood" said Hannah.

Back at St Meryl's. Rosie looked at her grandma.

"I mean you have been doing actually the same

to Auntie Sophie, Hannah and Maddie and she doesn't believe anymore because of you" said Rosie.

Chapter seven – Persuasive

Maddie looked at Zoe.

"Please, she's in trouble," said Zoe.

Maddie nodded.

Zoe led her further into Crystal Woods.

Back at St Meryl's, Grandma Elizabeth looked around for Maddie confused.

"Where's Madison-Rose?" asked Grandma Elizabeth.

Mrs Nicholas looked around.

"I have no idea" lied Mrs Nicholas

looking at her mum then her husband.

"Where is she?" he mouthed "Crystal Woods. Hannah's had a fall" Mrs Nicholas mouthed back but it wasn't as quiet as Mrs Nicholas thought.

"Maddie's going to Crystal Woods?" asked Grandma Elizabeth looking shocked.

In Crystal Woods, Maddie was walking further into Crystal Woods with Zoe.

"Why don't you believe in me anymore?" asked

Zoe "because you don't exist. You're not" Maddie stopped as soon as I saw Hannah.

"Hannah" Maddie shouted and ran up to my big sister.

Maddie bent down "are you okay? What happened?" asked Maddie.

Hannah and I looked at Maddie.

"What?" asked Maddie "what's going on with you mads?" I asked, "what do you mean?" asked Maddie "you didn't want go and see Zoe? That's not like you. Is it something to do with Grandma?" asked Hannah.

Maddie looked at Hannah.

"Please, tell me mads. I'm really

worried about you?" asked Hannah "I'm going to college, aren't I?" said Maddie.

"Oh, Mads. That doesn't mean you stop believing in Zoe" said Brooke "but Grandma" Maddie stopped.

Hannah looked at Maddie.

"Mads, listen to me okay. I'm going to uni, I'm engaged and I'm

21 but where am I?" asked Hannah "In Crystal Woods" said Maddie "who conceived me to believe again?" asked Hannah "me? I did" said

Maddie looking at Hannah.

"So?" asked Maddie "do you get my point? It's okay to believe. Don't worry about Grandma Elizabeth, okay?"

asked Hannah

"Okay Hannah-Banana," said Maddie.

Chapter eight- you win

"I'm glad that you are back to your old self Mads," said Hannah.

Maddie smiled when Brooke came running.

"Oh, you're back" I said hugging Maddie.

I smiled as I let go of Maddie.

"I'm sorry if I've been a bit grumpy lately. I'm waiting for a college confirmation letter" said Maddie "oh Mads, is it grandma

pressuring you?"
asked Hannah.

Maddie nodded.

"Right, come on
I've had enough"
said Hannah
grabbing my hand
but Maddie let go.

"Han, what are you doing?" asked Maddie "she's bullying you, I'm your big sister. It's my job to protect you" said Hannah grabbing Maddie's hand again and grabbed mine and we walked out of Crystal Woods and into St Meryl's and over to Grandma Elizabeth.

Maddie looked at me as Hannah

tapped Grandma Elizabeth.

Grandma Elizabeth turned around looking angry.

"Why are you trying to make

Madison back into believing in teddies?" asked Grandma Elizabeth "and why are you pressuring her to get into a good enough college?" asked Hannah "nothing is good enough for you is it?" she asked "I'm trying to pressure her to get into the same college as me" said Grandma Elizabeth.

As Grandma Elizabeth and Hannah continued arguing, Madison, Sophie, Michael, and I as Sophie had an envelope addressed to Madison.

Sophie looked at Madison.

"Is that the confirmation letter?" asked Madison "yeah" said Mrs Nicholas and gave Madison the envelope and she opened it.

Hannah looked over at us and came over with Grandma.

"What's that Mads?" asked

Hannah "the confirmation letter," said Madison.

They all went silent as Maddie peeled the envelope open ...

Chapter nine- You got in

Maddie took the folding piece of paper out of the envelope and unfolded it and read.

"So? Did you get in?" asked Hannah.

There was silent.

"Mads?" asked Brooke.

Maddie looked up smiling.

"Did you get in?" asked Mrs Nicholas.

Maddie nodded continuing.

Hannah jumped up with

excitement and ran up to Maddie.

"I'm so proud of you" said Hannah "well done sweetheart," said Mrs Nicholas.

Maddie looked around and I was nowhere to be seen "where's B?" asked Maddie "who?" asked Mr Nicholas "Brooke, that's her nickname daddy," said Maddie.

Mr Nicholas smiled "Ahh" he said.

Maddie looked around looking worried.

"What's up Mads?" asked Martha "have you seen B?" asked Maddie "no, I thought she was with you" said Martha "no, I've just got the confirmation letter that I got into college" said Maddie "well done Mads" said Martha "thanks, Mart. I'm going to have a look and see if she's gone to Crystal Woods" said Maddie

"Crystal Woods? What's that?" asked Martha.

Maddie looked at Martha.

"it's umm" said Maddie and looked over at

Mrs and Mr Nicholas and ran off towards them.

"Maddie, what's wrong?" asked Hannah.

I started panicking and walking up and down.

Lily and Martha came running and at this point, I was in the middle of a panic attack.

"What's up with mads?" asked Lily
"I don't know, breathe and try and relax," said Hannah.

Maddie relaxed and her breathing calmed down.

"Right, what's up mads?" asked Hannah smiling.

Maddie looked at Hannah sad.

"Brooke's gone missing," said Maddie

Printed in Great Britain
by Amazon

32246871R00089